OG'S ARK

For Elliot and Claire — A. and W. Marks
For my Nephew — M.P.

Text copyright © 2016 by Allison and Wayne Marks
Illustrations copyright © 2016 Lerner Publishing Group, Inc.

KAR-BEN PUBLISHING
A division of Lerner Publishing Group, Inc.
241 First Avenue North
Minneapolis, MN 55401 USA
1-800-4-KARBEN

Website address: www.karben.com

Main body text set in ChurchwardSamoa 17/22.
Typeface provided by Chank.

Library of Congress Cataloging-in-Publication Data

Marks, Allison, author.
    Og's ark / by Allison Marks & Wayne Marks ; illustrated by Martina Peluso.
      pages cm
    Summary: "Og the giant is a friend to many animals, but is otherwise grumpy because he can't find a bed big enough to support him. Noah enlists Og's help gathering animals for the ark, and in return, Og is rewarded with an iron bed that allows him to finally sleep"— Provided by publisher.
      ISBN 978-1-4677-6149-9 (lb : alk. paper) —
      ISBN 978-1-4677-6150-5 (pb : alk. paper) —
      [1. Giants—Fiction. 2. Noah's ark—Fiction. 3. Beds—Fiction. 4. Sleep—Fiction.] I. Marks, Wayne, author. II. Peluso, Martina, illustrator. III. Title.
    PZ7.1.M372Og 2016
    [E]—dc23   2015016341

Manufactured in the United States of America
1 - VP - 7/15/16

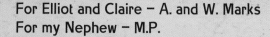

OG'S ARK

Allison and Wayne Marks

Illustrated by Martina Peluso

KAR-BEN
PUBLISHING

In olden times, after God separated the earth from the sky, Og the Giant came into the world.

Before the sun set on Og's first day, all in the land realized he was no ordinary baby.

When Og cried, entire forests swayed and villagers miles away covered their ears to block out the noise.

The sound of his cooing echoed in the canyons and caused boulders to tumble from the highest mountaintop.

Buckets of milk gathered from one hundred cows and one hundred goats barely satisfied Og's hunger.

Og's first bed, a cradle built from the finest oak, shattered into a million pieces under his weight. As time passed, Og turned many more beds into piles of splinters.

Og grew . . . and grew . . . and grew . . . until his shoulders touched the top of the tallest cedar tree. Now no bed in the land could hold him.

Without a bed, Og struggled to sleep on the hard ground under the stars. When it rained, Og was too wet and cold to catch a moment's rest.

After each night of tossing and turning, Og grew grumpier. His earth-shaking yawns and bleary eyes made people tremble with fear. But the animals knew that under Og's gruffness beat the heart of a gentle giant.

At dusk, animals gathered from far and wide, seeking a safe place to spend the night.

Chickadees and sparrows nested in Og's bushy beard. Chipmunks and woodchucks burrowed inside his pockets. Raccoons and flying squirrels rested in the crooks of his arms. Black bears and moose curled at his feet.

All was peaceful and quiet ... but not for long.

The parrots talked in their sleep. The hyenas cackled at their own jokes. Yaks yakked. Lions roared. Donkeys brayed. Rabbits twitched. Wolves could be heard counting sheep, while sheep could be heard counting wolves.

Eventually, everyone nodded off to sleep ...

Except Og.

As the seasons passed, a wise man named Noah noticed how kindly Og treated the animals. One day, Noah approached the giant.

"Why have you come here?" Og bellowed. He was especially tired and grouchy that morning.

"A Great Flood is coming soon," Noah told Og.

"How does this concern me?" Og asked. "I am so tall that no flood can drown me."

"God's other creatures are not so lucky," replied Noah. "God has told me to build an ark and fill it with a male and female of every animal. I have seen how the animals love and trust you. Will you help bring them to the ark?"

Og agreed.

Og traveled near and far gathering a pair of every living creature. A parade of animals, two by two, followed Og's giant footsteps all the way to the ark. Albatrosses and alligators. Ostriches and orangutans. Toucans and tigers. Sloths and scorpions. Walruses and woodpeckers.

Og helped each animal board the ark,
from the tiniest vole to the tallest giraffe.

Once the zebras trotted into the great ship, Og bent down to enter but he could not fit through the door.

Head bowed and eyes filled with tears, Og turned to walk away. "Wait," Noah called, "There is room on top of the ark where you can ride out the storm. Won't you join us?"

Sleeping on the rough ground had been hard for Og, but spending forty nights straddling the ark was even harder. Rain pelted him. The howling winds made sleep impossible. Og's growling stomach rang in his ears and chased away his dreams. But in spite of it all, Og took comfort in every mooooo!, squawk!, and hisssss! he heard from his friends safely below.

At last, the Great Flood ended. All the animals returned to their burrows, caves, and nests.

Noah thanked Og for his help. "You have been a good friend to the animals," Noah said. "How can I repay you?"

"All I want is a good night's sleep in my own bed," Og sighed.

Noah stroked his beard, looked up to the heavens, and said, "Perhaps God will reward you for your good deed."

Og set off on his own, wondering what Noah had meant. As night fell, he came upon a magnificent palace unlike any he had ever seen.

When he stepped inside, Og could barely believe his eyes. Before him stood an enormous bed made of iron.

The headboard reached to the ceiling and the plumpest pillows awaited Og's weary head. He smoothed his hands over the soft sheets and bent down to examine each of the bed's sturdy legs.

As slowly as he could, Og lowered himself onto the edge of the bed. He held his breath, waiting for a loud crash. But none came. For the first time in Og's life, a bed held strong. "This is what I've always wanted! Thank you!" he cried, looking up.

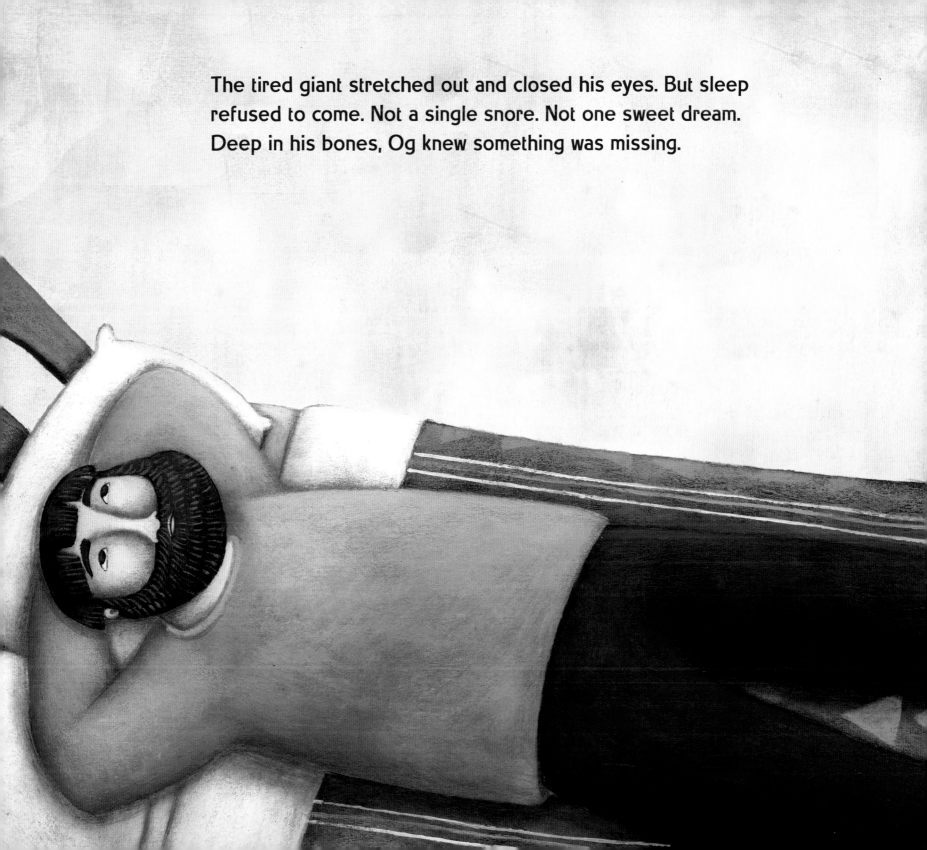

The tired giant stretched out and closed his eyes. But sleep refused to come. Not a single snore. Not one sweet dream. Deep in his bones, Og knew something was missing.

Suddenly, thunderclaps shook the palace. Boom! Boom! Boom! Rain drummed against the palace roof.

In the distance, Og heard another sound—the approaching rumble of pounding hooves and flapping wings.

Frightened by the storm, animals raced two by two into the palace.

Bats and bison. Elks and echidnas. Herons and hippopotamuses. Llamas and lobsters. Peacocks and platypuses. Everyone found a place aboard Og's iron bed.

All was peaceful and quiet ...

But not for long.

Mice squeaked. Elephants trumpeted. Pigs hogged the blankets.

And one very happy giant laughed. Eventually, everyone nodded off to sleep.

Even Og.

Authors' Note

Og, the last of the giants, is based on the biblical character of Og, the King of Bashan. It is said that, due to his enormous size, Og was unable to fit into the ark so he survived the Great Flood by holding onto the roof. The Book of *Devarim* mentions Og's iron bed as measuring "nine cubits in length and four cubits in breadth," which is about six feet wide and thirteen feet long. "Og's Ark" blends the tale of Noah and the Flood with the biblical reference to the giant's bed.